MW00949167

BEWARE! THIS SPOOKY

BELONGS TO

____

NLY THE BRAVEST LITTLE MONSTERS CAN COLOR THESE PAGES!

GRAB YOUR MAGICAL CRAYONS AND GET READY TO MAKE THESE HALLOWEEN SCENES COME ALIVE—IF YOU DARE!

CRAYON TESTING ZONE

EFORE YOU DIVE INTO THE SPOOKY FUN, USE THIS PAGE TO TEST OUT YOUR COLORS!

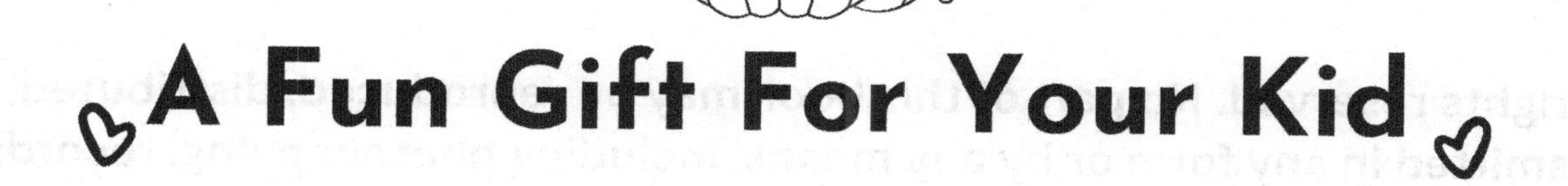

A Fun Gift For Your Kid

Thank you a ton for snagging this awesome coloring book!

As an added bonus, I've got some super fun FREEBIES for your little one to grab and have a blast with.

Instructions:

1. ***Open the camera on your phone (as if you're going to take a photo).***
2. ***Hold the phone over the QR code below.***
3. ***A link will appear on your screen.***
4. ***Tap on the link to get your free download!***

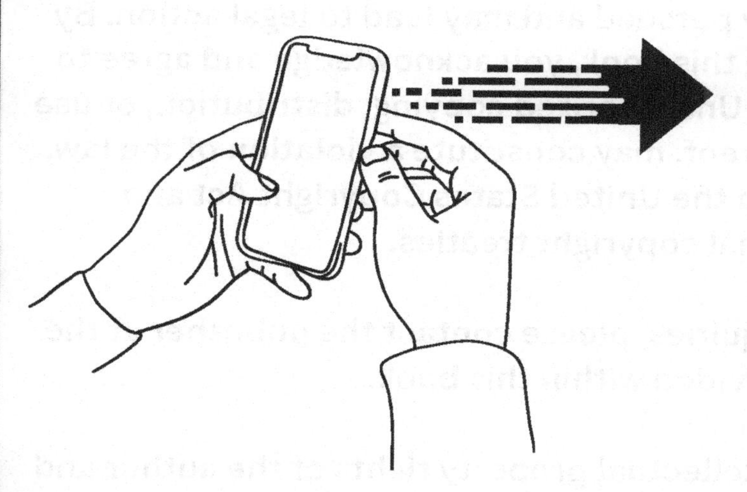

If you don't see the email in your inbox within a few minutes, please check your spam folder just in case it got lost along the way.

With deep appreciation,
Christian Garrett

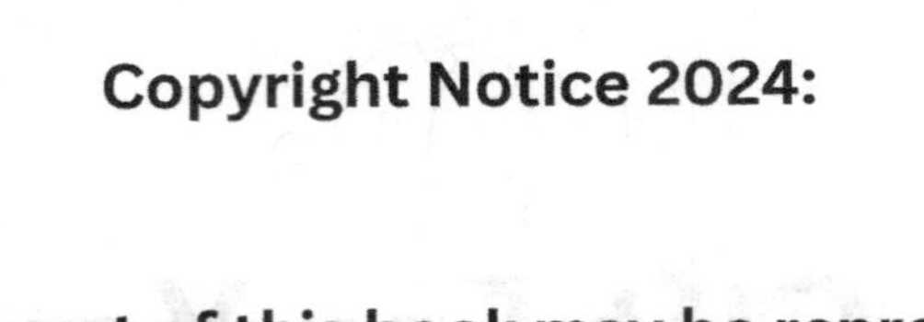

Copyright Notice 2024:

All rights reserved. No part of this book may be reproduced, distributed, or transmitted in any form or by any means, including photocopying, recording, or other electronic or mechanical methods, without the prior written permission of the publisher, except in the case of brief quotations embodied in critical reviews and certain other noncommercial uses permitted by copyright law.

This book is intended solely for personal and non-commercial use. The information, ideas, concepts, characters, plots, illustrations, and any other elements contained within this book are protected by copyright laws and international treaties. Any unauthorized use, reproduction, or distribution of these materials is strictly prohibited and may result in civil and criminal penalties under applicable laws.

Readers are hereby informed that any infringement of the copyright terms stated herein will be vigorously pursued and may lead to legal action. By purchasing, accessing, or using this book, you acknowledge and agree to abide by these copyright terms. Unauthorized copying, distribution, or use of this book, or any portion thereof, may constitute a violation of the law, including but not limited to the United States Copyright Act and international copyright treaties.

For permissions requests or inquiries, please contact the publisher at the address provided within this book.

Thank you for respecting the intellectual property rights of the author and publisher.

Christian Garrett 2024

HALLOWEEN DATE:
Halloween is celebrated on October 31st
every year.

ORIGIN OF HALLOWEEN:
The word "Halloween" comes from "All Hallows' Eve," which means the evening before All Saints' Day.

JACK-O'-LANTERNS:
People carve pumpkins into Jack-o'-lanterns to
light up the night on Halloween.

R.I.P.
R.I.P.
R.I.P.
R.I.P.

PUMPKIN COLORS:

Pumpkins are usually orange, but they can also be white, green, or even blue!

COSTUME TRADITION:
The tradition of wearing costumes on Halloween
comes from ancient people who dressed up to
scare away ghosts.

HALLOWEEN BATS:
Bats are often associated with Halloween
because they come out at night.

R.I.P

BLACK CAT MAGIC:
Black cats are considered good luck in some cultures, but on Halloween, they're seen as mysterious and magical.

CANDY CORN HISTORY:
Candy corn is one of the most popular Halloween treats and was invented over 100 years ago.

TRICK-OR-TREATING BEGINS:
Trick-or-treating started in the United States in the 1920s.

HAUNTED HOUSES:
Haunted houses are a popular attraction during Halloween, where people go to get a little scared.

GIANT PUMPKIN RECORD:
The largest pumpkin ever grown weighed over
2,700 pounds!

ANOTHER NAME FOR HALLOWEEN:
In some places, Halloween is also known as "All Hallows' Eve."

BOO

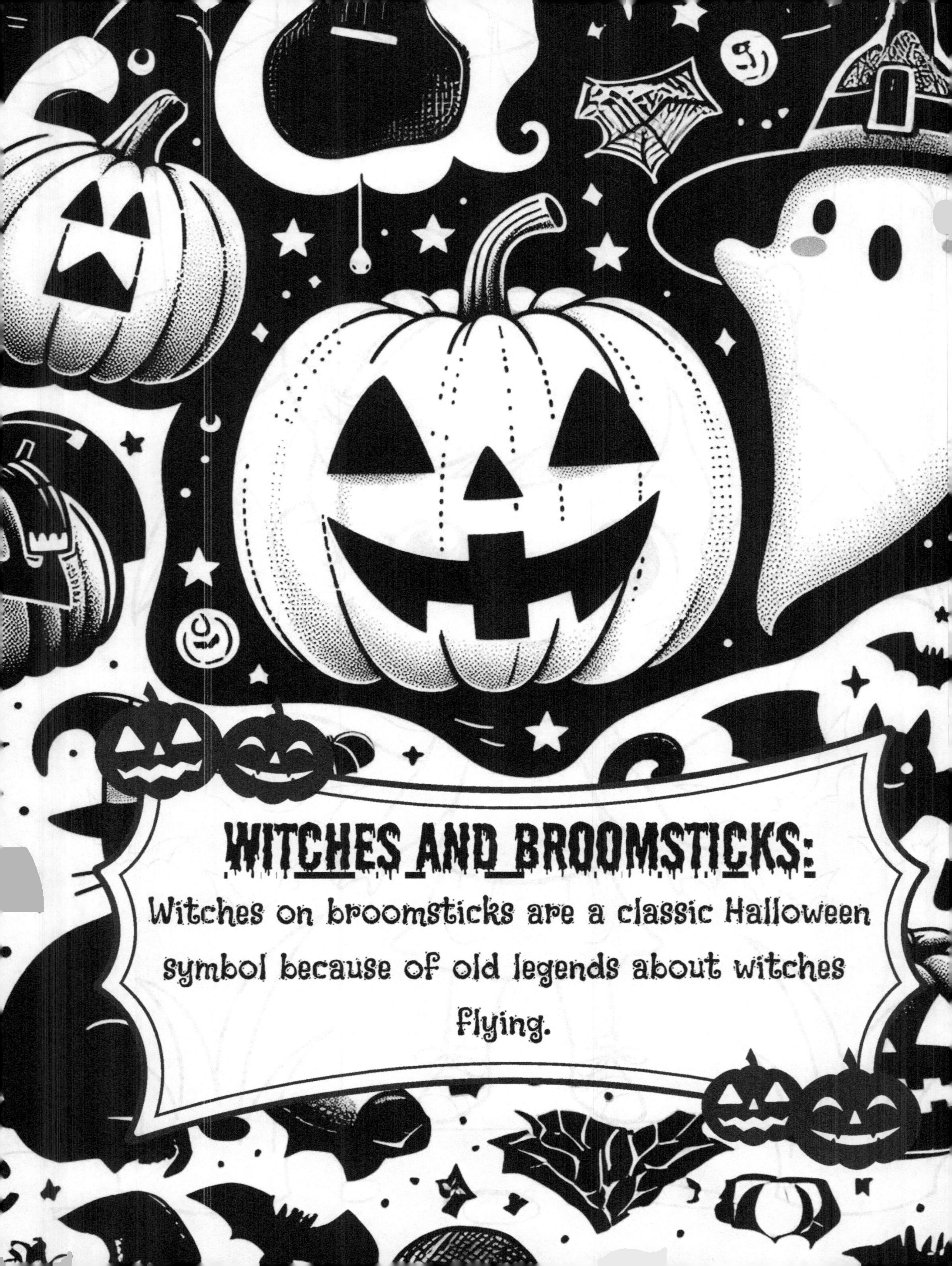
WITCHES AND BROOMSTICKS:
Witches on broomsticks are a classic Halloween symbol because of old legends about witches flying.

SPOOKY SKELETONS:
Skeletons are popular Halloween decorations
because they represent the spirit world.

GHOSTLY HALLOWEEN:
Ghosts are believed to come out on Halloween night because it's the time when the boundary between the living and the dead is the thinnest.

Happy
Halloween

VAMPIRE LEGENDS:
Vampire legends come from old stories about creatures that drink blood to stay alive.

LUCKY SPIDERS:
Some people believe that seeing a spider on Halloween is good luck because it means a loved one is watching over you.

MUMMY WRAPS:
Mummies are wrapped-up bodies from ancient Egypt, but on Halloween, they're spooky fun!

HALLOWEEN COLORS:
The color orange represents the fall harvest,
and black represents the darkness of night.

TRICK OR TREAT

OWL MYTHS:

Owls are associated with Halloween because they are night birds and were once believed to be witches in disguise.

SAMHAIN FESTIVAL:
In Ireland, Halloween was originally called "Samhain," a festival marking the end of the harvest season.

HALLOWEEN LIGHTS:
Some families hang up Halloween lights, just like Christmas lights, to decorate their homes.

CANDY APPLES:
Candy apples are a sweet Halloween treat made
by dipping apples in sugary syrup.

APPLE BOBBING FUN:
Many people play games like bobbing for apples at Halloween parties.

CHARLIE BROWN AND HALLOWEEN:
The movie "It's the Great Pumpkin, Charlie Brown" is a Halloween favorite.

TRICK OR TREAT

SCARECROW SIGHTINGS:
Scarecrows are often seen during Halloween because they protect crops in the fall.

NIGHT CREATURES:

Some animals, like bats and spiders, are more active at night, making them perfect Halloween symbols.

COSTUME FAVORITES:
Many kids dress up as their favorite
superheroes or princesses for Halloween.

DECORATING FOR HALLOWEEN:
Halloween is the second most popular holiday
for decorating, after Christmas.

BOOOO!

TOP HALLOWEEN CANDY:
The most popular Halloween candy is chocolate, with Snickers and Reese's being top favorites.

DAY OF THE DEAD:
In Mexico, Halloween is celebrated as "Dia de los Muertos," or Day of the Dead, where families remember loved ones who have passed away.

STINGY JACK LEGEND:
Jack-o'-lanterns got their name from an old Irish legend about a man named "Stingy Jack."

RINGING BELLS:
Some people believe that ringing a bell on
Halloween night will scare away evil spirits.

COSTUME DISGUISE:
Wearing a costume on Halloween helps to disguise you from any ghosts that might be around!

TEAL PUMPKIN PROJECT:
Some people put out a teal pumpkin to show they have non-food treats for kids with allergies.

WEREWOLF TALES:
Werewolves are legendary creatures that turn into wolves during a full moon.

B

HALLOWEEN BONFIRES:
In some countries, people make bonfires on Halloween to keep away bad spirits.

TRICK-OR-TREAT ORIGINS:
The tradition of trick-or-treating comes from "souling," where people would go door-to-door asking for food in exchange for prayers.

FUNNY PUMPKINS:
Some people carve funny faces into their pumpkins instead of scary ones to make people smile.

SPOOKY STORIES:
Halloween is a time for telling spooky stories,
but remember—they're just pretend!

HALLOWEEN SPENDING:
In the United States, people spend billions of dollars every year on Halloween candy and costumes.

SAYING 'BOO!':
"Boo" is a fun way to surprise someone on Halloween!

ANOKA HALLOWEEN:
The first city to officially celebrate Halloween
was Anoka, Minnesota, in 1920.

LUCKY BATS:
Some people believe that bats are lucky because
they eat bugs that can harm crops.

DIY COSTUMES:

You can make your own Halloween costume at home with things you already have!

FULL MOON FRIGHT:
A full moon on Halloween is rare but makes the night extra spooky.

GLOW-IN-THE-DARK COSTUMES:
Some Halloween costumes glow in the dark so kids can be seen easily at night.

HALLOWEEN FUN!:
Halloween is a time for fun, laughter, and a
little bit of spookiness—but it's all in good fun!

HALLOWEEN SONGS:
Some Halloween songs, like "Monster Mash," are popular tunes that people love to sing and dance to during the spooky season.

PUMPKIN SPICE:
Pumpkin spice, a mix of cinnamon, nutmeg, and cloves, is a favorite Halloween flavor found in treats like lattes, cookies, and cakes!

CONGRATULATIONS!

THIS CERTIFIES THAT ______________________

HAS SUCCESSFULLY COMPLETED THE "JUMBO HALLOWEEN COLORING BOOK FOR KIDS!" YOU'VE DONE AN AMAZING JOB BRINGING THESE HALLOWEEN SCENES TO LIFE WITH YOUR CREATIVITY AND COLORS.

KEEP UP THE GREAT WORK AND CONTINUE TO EXPLORE THE MAGICAL WORLD OF ART!

DATE:

____

Christian Garrett
____

Made in the USA
Monee, IL
28 October 2024